D0116470

Purchased from
Multnomah County Library
Title Wave Used Bookstore
216 NE Knott St, Portland, OR
503-988-5021

Mary Smith, 1927

MARY SMITH

Andrea U'Ren

Farrar, Straus and Giroux
New York

To Mary Smith, herself

Thanks to Sebastian, Sean, Carol Healy, and Dad.
And especially to Mom—who introduced me to Mary.

Copyright © 2003 by Andrea U'Ren. All rights reserved. Distributed in Canada by Douglas
& McIntyre Ltd. Color separations by Hong Kong Scanner Arts. Printed and bound in the
United States of America by Berryville Graphics. Designed by Jennifer Crilly. First edition, 2003
10 9 8 7 6 5 4 3 2 1

Photograph of Mary Smith, page 1, Topham / The Image Works; photograph of anonymous
knocker-up, page 32, collection of the author.

Library of Congress Cataloging-in-Publication Data
U'Ren, Andrea.
    Mary Smith / Andrea U'Ren.— 1st ed.
        p.   cm.
    Summary: Early in the morning Mary Smith walks through the town, waking people up by
shooting at their windows with her peashooter.
    ISBN 0-374-34842-1
    [1. City and town life—Fiction.   2. Sleep—Fiction.   3. Morning—Fiction.]   I. Title.

PZ7.U66 Mar 2003
[E]—dc21   2002069775

It's Monday morning, hours before dawn, and Mary Smith, the knocker-up, has left her home. She walks for miles from the outskirts of town, passing one sleeping house after another . . .

. . . then suddenly stops. She takes one
dried pea (wrinkly!) from her pocket and
puts it into her peashooter.

   Then . . .

TINK! She's hit the baker's window!

TOK! She hits it again!

On goes a light.
"I'M AWAKE!"
the baker shouts, sleepily.
"All right?"

But Mary Smith doesn't respond. She's already gone.

Look!
Here she is hurrying along,
the baker's home far behind.
Then . . .

. . . she stops again—in front of the
train conductor's home, this time.

  She hits his window with one pea.
TINK!

  Then hits it with two more.
CLACK! DINK!

The train conductor comes to
the window, but then he falls
asleep again!
So . . .

. . . Mary blows and gently flicks his nose.

"Hup, yup!" He yawns and turns on a light. "See? I'm up!"

But Mary Smith's already
on her way—and waking up
the laundry maids
(*TOCK! TOCK! TOCK!*)
and the fishmonger
(*PLIK PLOK!*).

All through town, Mary Smith shoots dried peas to rouse sleeping townspeople . . .

. . . so they can start their day on time.

And finally, at the end of Edgeton Lane,
the mayor's windows crackle with
a *CLICK CLACK SNAP!*

No one comes to the window. So Mary tries again: *TOK TOK CLACK!*

The windows swing open.

"It must be my turn to wake up," the mayor says.

"That's right," says Mary Smith with pride. "The other townspeople are already up."

"Without you," says the mayor, wiping sleep from his eyes, "everyone would still be asleep in bed, no one would be working, and I wouldn't have a town to run— because everything would be shut down!

"So, thank you, Mary Smith. I don't know what we'd do without you!

"See you tomorrow morning, right?"

"Dim and early!" Mary says with a grin.

Here's Mary Smith eating a warm bun, fresh from the bakery. She hears the whistle of the 7:07 train, which—as always—is leaving exactly on time.

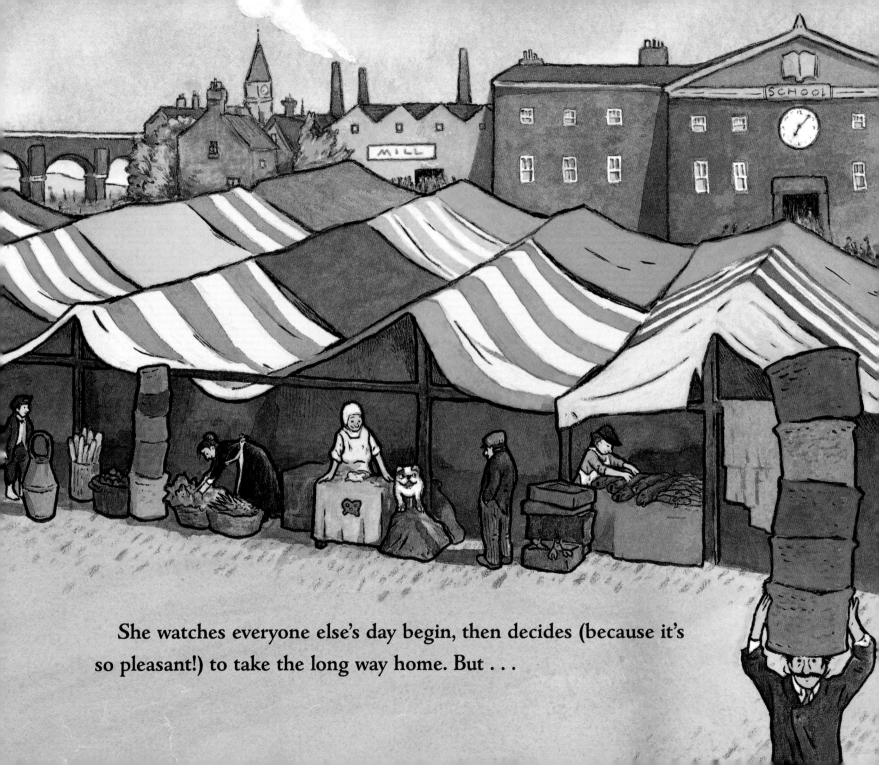

She watches everyone else's day begin, then decides (because it's so pleasant!) to take the long way home. But . . .

. . . when Mary Smith arrives back home, she finds a dreadful sight!

Is that really her daughter sound asleep in bed, so *very late* for school?

"Rose! Wake up!" cries Mary Smith. "Oh! How impossible it will be to get anyone to wake up for me after they hear about *this*— my *own* daughter sleeping in!"

"I'm not late for school, Mummy," answers Rose, sadly. "It's worse than that! I've been sent home. Timothy was sleeping, so I tried to wake him up . . .

. . . but I missed and hit Miss Pinchitt instead."

"For SHAME!" gasps Mary Smith.

"We really must work on your aim!"

A Way to Wake Up

Before alarm clocks were affordable and reliable, people needed a way to wake up on time. This was especially true when people started working in mills and factories,

because shifts often began very early in the morning. In England, one solution to this problem was to hire someone called a "knocker-up." For a few pennies a week, a knocker-up would come around to wake you at whatever time you requested.

The real Mrs. Mary Smith, from the East End of London, shot dried peas from a hard rubber tube to wake her clients, but most other knocker-ups used long lightweight poles with wires attached at the end. The knocker-up would reach the pole up to your bedroom window and tap or scratch away. It must have made quite a racket! You had to go to the window and show the knocker-up you were awake before he or she would move on to the next house.